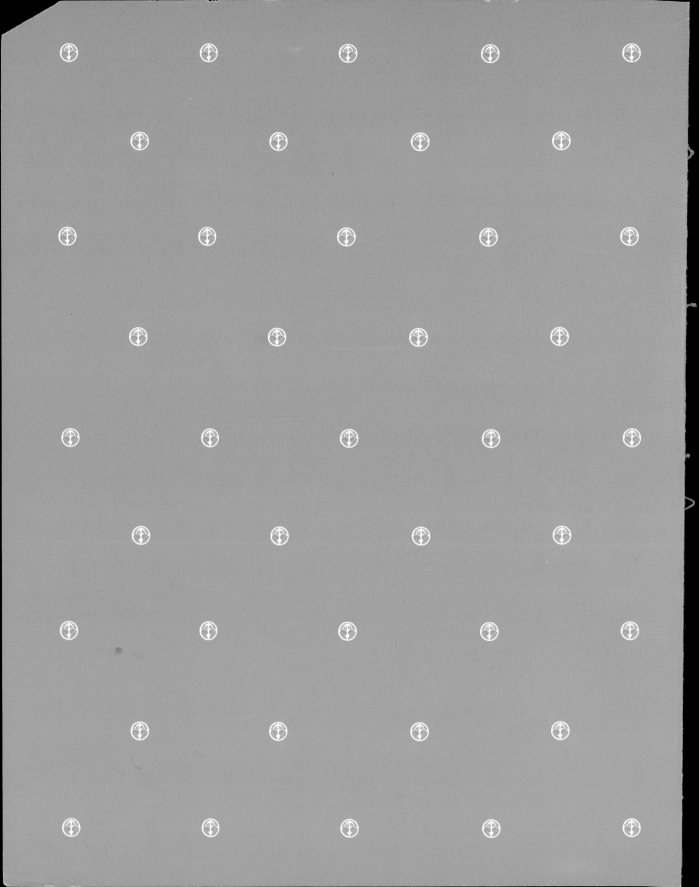

Obon

by Ruth Suyenaga

Illustrated by
Yoshi Miyake

MULTICULTURAL CELEBRATIONS II

MODERN CURRICULUM PRESS

Multicultural Celebrations was created under the auspices of

The Children's Museum, Boston.
Leslie Swartz, Director of Teacher Services,
directed this project.

Design: Gary Fujiwara
Photographs: 6, Don Smetzer/TSW; 14, Consulate
General of Japan/ISEI; 21, Courtesy of Midwest Buddhist
Temple, Chicago, IL

MODERN CURRICULUM PRESS, INC.
13900 Prospect Road
Cleveland, Ohio 44136

ISBN 0-8136-2321-9 (soft cover)   0-8136-2322-7 (hard cover)

1 2 3 4 5 6 7 8 9 10   97 96 95 94 93

Simon & Schuster   A Paramount Communications Company

Maile sat back in her airplane seat. She thought of the day she had come home saying…"Mom! Softball tryouts are July 1st."

"But on July 1st we'll be on a plane to Hawaii," her Mom had said. "Uncle Mark just sent us tickets to come for the family reunion and the Japanese *Obon* festival."

1

"Hawaii? *Obon* festival?" Maile had asked. "What about the tryouts...?"

"I'm sorry, dear, you'll have to miss them. But, you will get to meet your cousin Kim. She's just your age."

So Maile had not been happy to get on the plane. When they landed, Aunty Karen and her other relatives had met Maile and her Mom and Dad. But Kim hadn't been very friendly and there didn't seem to be anyone else Maile's age.

"I guess I should be glad to be here," she told her Mom. "But Hawaii seems so different from Massachusetts. And Kim hasn't even talked to me much. All I can think about is being back home... and playing softball."

"Give it time," her Mom said. "I think Kim is just shy."

2

The next night the whole family went to one of the *Obon* festivals. Aunty Karen explained the festivals are held at *Buddhist* temples. The excitement of the event surprised Maile. Her hometown didn't have any *Buddhist* temples, or many Japanese American families either.

Maile stood with her Dad watching Kim's brother strike a *taiko* drum. Aunty Karen and Maile wore *yukatas*, cotton *kimonos*.

"Come and join us," she laughed, pulling Maile into a circle of dancers. "It's the *Kyushu Tanko Bushi*, the traditional coal miners' dance."

Maile tried to follow as the dancers swayed their arms and stamped their feet. She was caught up in the steady beat of the *taiko* drum.

"I know everything here seems strange to you," Aunty Karen
said. "And I don't know what's gotten into that Kim!
But you and I can get into the spirit of *Obon*."

"What is the festival all about?" Maile asked.

"It's a time of year to remember our ancestors. We
think about our relatives who have died and all they
have taught us. Some *Buddhists* believe that the spirits
of their ancestors visit at *Obon*. They welcome them with
incense and *mochi* — rice cakes. They put flowers
on their ancestors' graves and have special temple
services for them."

6

Aunty Karen continued. "It is believed that on the third evening of *Obon*, the spirits of the ancestors leave. They are guided by floating paper lanterns. In fact, it's ten o'clock now. Let's go down to the shore."

Maile followed the crowd to the water. Hundreds of lanterns flickered in the night.

"The long boat with all the flowers is called the mother boat." Aunty Karen handed her a lantern. "This one has the name of *O-jii-chan*, your great-grandfather, on it. You can put it into the water.

"You know, we have pictures of your relatives in great-grandmother's photo album. I can show them to you tomorrow."

Maile thought about her ancestors. She waded into the water and set off her lantern, watching it drift slowly out to sea.

The next morning at breakfast, Maile decided to try one more time to get to know Kim.

"The lanterns were beautiful last night," Maile said to her cousin.

"H-m-m-m," Kim answered, not looking up.

"Kim... Maile," interrupted Aunty Karen coming into the kitchen with Maile's Mom. "Help us prepare the guava cake, potato salad, and *sashimi*."

That began a day of cooking for the family reunion picnic. Kim and Maile worked side by side.

They couldn't help laughing as they all ran into each other working in the crowded kitchen.

"Time to make the *musubi*," Aunty Karen said close to noon.

13

"OK," Maile answered, "But I don't know how."

"Haven't you made rice balls before? " Kim asked surprised. "I thought you'd know everything, coming from the mainland."

"We don't have an *Obon* festival back home. You're lucky."

"Here, let me help you," Kim said smiling. She and Maile took some warm rice and tucked in the *ume* — the tart pickled plum. Then they wrapped it with a strip of *nori* — seaweed.

"Girls. I hear your *O-bah-chan* calling," said Aunty Karen. "Please go see what your great-grandmother *wants*."

O-bah-chan couldn't speak much English, but they could communicate with her.

"Great! *O-bah-chan* has the family photo album out," Kim said.

"Oh, the photos," said Maile. "I almost forgot. Aunty Karen said I could look at them."

O-bah-chan turned the pages as the girls looked with interest at the faces of their relatives.

"I haven't added my favorite picture of myself yet. We all get to do that," said Kim. "*O-bah-chan*, I think I'll go get my photo. OK?" Their great-grandmother nodded.

"Do you have a picture to put in the album, Maile?"

"I think I do. I brought along a picture of myself in my favorite outfit," she said running out of the room.

The girls returned, placing their pictures in front of *O-bah-chan* at the same time. They gasped in surprise. Both photos showed smiling softball teams.

"You play softball?" Kim asked.

"Sure, I play first base," Maile answered. "And you?"

"I'm the pitcher."

"Well, then you'll know how I feel right now. The team tryouts..." said Maile starting to tell Kim the whole story.

"Kim... telephone," her mother called, just at that moment. "It's your coach."

18

"Oh, NO!" Maile heard Kim yell into the phone as Maile joined her in the kitchen. "Randy broke her arm? Ah, shucks! Isn't there someone else who could play?" Kim pleaded.

"Wait a minute, Coach..." Kim said as she gave Maile a thumbs' up sign. "I just happen to know a great softball player who isn't busy this afternoon."

Maile looked at her — frowned for a minute — and then smiled.

Maybe this *Obon* and family reunion weren't so bad after all.

Glossary

Buddhist (BOOD-ihst) a believer in the religion based on the teachings of Buddha

kimono (KEE-MOE-noh) a traditional Japanese robe, usually made of silk

mochi (MOH-CHEE) pounded rice cakes made from steamed rice that are served at Japanese celebrations

musubi (moo-SOO-bee) rice balls often wrapped with seaweed

nori (NOH-ree) very thin seaweed

O-bah-chan (oh-BAH-chahn) grandmother or great-grandmother

Obon (oh BOHN) Buddhist day to remember the dead

O-jii-chan (oh-JEE-chahn) grandfather or great-grandfather

sashimi (SA-SHEE-MEE) slices of raw fish eaten with soy sauce

taiko (TIE-ko) a large, barrel-shaped drum

ume (OO-may) a tart, pickled plum

yukata (yoo KAH tah) cotton Japanese robe worn in the summer

22

About the Author

Ruth Suyenaga is a classroom teacher who conducts workshops on Asian Americans and multicultural education. She is a *sansei* (third generation Japanese American) born in Hawaii. She dedicates this story to her daughter Maile and son Kenji. Ruth Suyenaga co-authored *Korean Children's Day.*

About the Illustrator

Yoshi Miyake was born in Tokyo, Japan. She came to the United States to study art at the American Academy of Art in Chicago. She is the illustrator of many children's books and has a special interest in Native Americans and their art. This is the first book Yoshi has illustrated that is about her own culture.